For Craig Smith,
our very own Bear
J. G. & M. W.

For Sam
A. J.

BEAR MAKE DEN

NOW MAKE DEN

STORY BY
Jane Godwin
& Michael Wagner

PICTURES BY
Andrew Joyner

CANDLEWICK PRESS

Bear make den.

Den good.

Den great.

Den just right.

Den not done.

Den need...

chairs!

Wait.

Den need...

table!

Den still not right!

Den need...

bed.

Den need…

sofa.

Den too dark.

Den need…

light.

Bear hungry.

Bear need...

cake!

Den need…

game.

Den need...

art.

Den done.

Candlewick Press, 99 Dover Street, Somerville, Massachusetts 02144. visit us at www.candlewick.com
Printed in Shenzhen, Guangdong, China.   17 18 19 20 21 22 CCP 10 9 8 7 6 5 4 3 2 1

FSC
www.fsc.org

MIX
Paper from
responsible sources
FSC® C008047